WEAKEND

_hydrus

Published by: Hydrus
Photography & Illustrated Art by: Hydrus
Cover Design by: Cleo Moran - Devoted Pages Designs
Formatting by: Cleo Moran - Devoted Pages Designs
https://www.devotedpages.com
Proofreading: Amina Jojo Dahmouche

Manufactured in the United States of America

The Library of Congress Cataloging-in-Publication Data is available upon request.

Paperback ISBN: 979-8-9856109-4-9

Dedicated to those of us
Who were mended only to be broken
_H

WeakEND

What happens when life and love clash?
When desire is blinding and passion betrays?
Who do you become and where does it all END?

Welcome to WeakEND, the first book in the FallEND
series.
Where we discover a man's journey to answer these
questions.

"Love gave so it could take" and only his inner
demons will keep him from his angels.

_hydrus

ONE WAY
ONE WAY
ON

I nèver knew life would crumble me again
hydrus

Bells and sirens
Knocking doors
Footsteps chatter
Squeaky floors

Eyes can't focus
Body aches
What's this place
Where I awake

Seems the shower
Plays the pipes
A bricked decor
With neon lights

Where am I now
Who am I with
My head is spinning
I have to sit

Alarmed
_hydrus

I
Keep
Falling
From
Myself

_hydrus

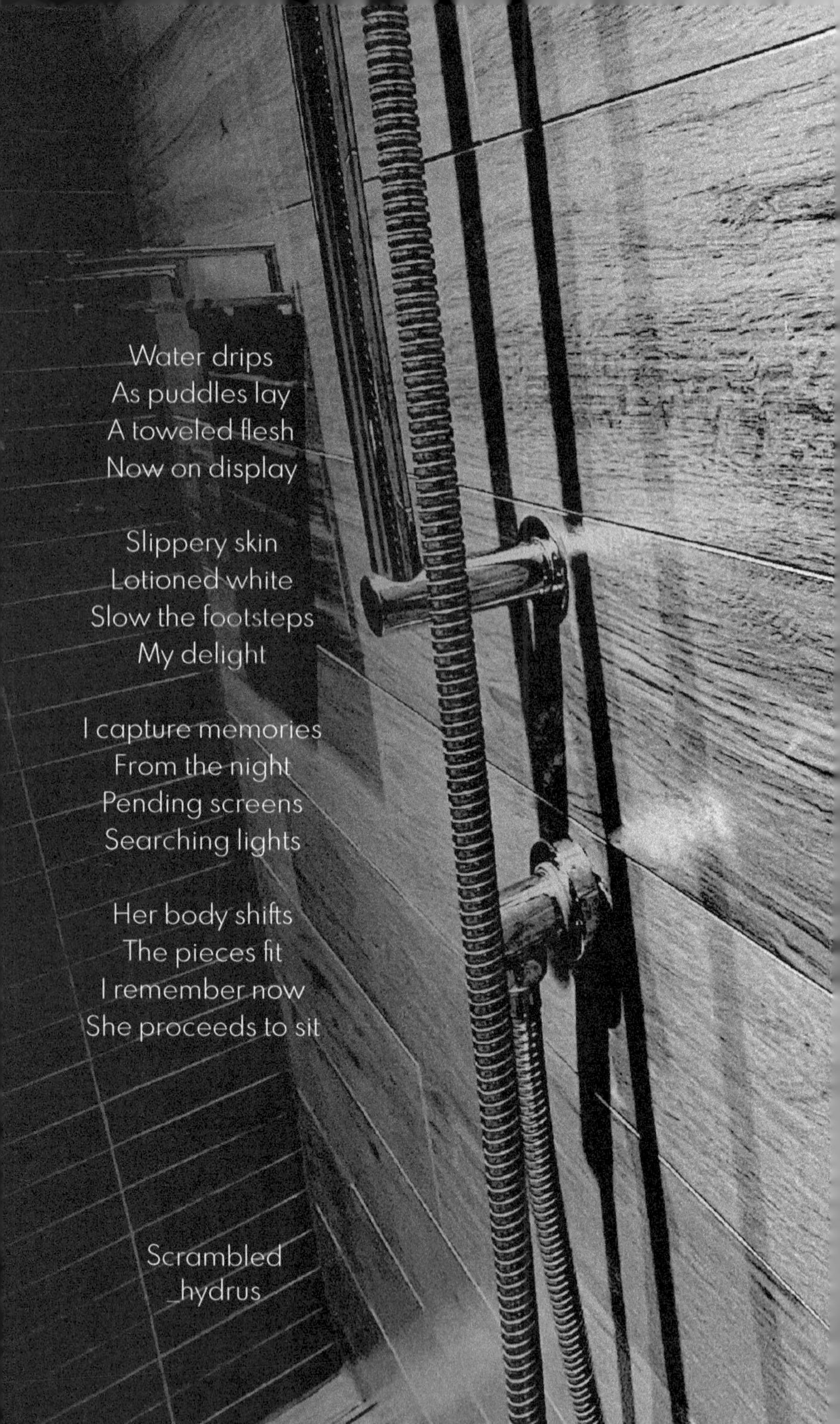

Water drips
As puddles lay
A toweled flesh
Now on display

Slippery skin
Lotioned white
Slow the footsteps
My delight

I capture memories
From the night
Pending screens
Searching lights

Her body shifts
The pieces fit
I remember now
She proceeds to sit

Scrambled
_hydrus

Flesh on flesh
I begin to drown
She takes me in
As we lay down

Every movement
Her body makes
Creates the hunger
Of my mistakes

Nothing on
She grabs my belt
Pulls me out
I begin to melt

Slowly lapping
Her mouth my hole
Explode while moaning
I lose control

Reminded
_hydrus

Leave your scent as we swallow our souls
_hydrus

Savage hunger
Groans are wild
Our lust is raw
So volatile

We just met
All clothes are torn
Between her legs
I feel reborn

We thrash and choke
She begs and pleads
Licks her lips
Drips over me

Consuming flesh
Devouring skin
A wrestled mess
Of bliss and sin

Untamed the lust
Released the waves
I will not trust
I am okay

One Night
_hydrus

Iron sunset
Paints the sky
I retrace my steps
A gutted sigh

I make my way
Down these streets
A disheveled soul
Never at peace

I forgot her name
The poison sticks
Just another game
I'm out of tricks

Please find my way
Back to my home
Another day
To be alone

Walk
_hydrus

Subway
Eighth Ave
I can't find my way back to where I really never was
hydrus

Vinyl seats
Where the plastic shines
Worn out edges
Torn over time

This is my carriage
A shallow ride
Picked me up
So I could hide

Giving directions
When I'm truly lost
The wind is endless
I forget the cost

Another night
Now has to end
I need to change
Can't just pretend

Taxi
_hydrus

Temptation plots my course
As lust leaves me with remorse
_hydrus

Why must this happen
Am I just plagued
I act a role
Just to get laid

I need her back
I can't go on
My broken heart
I was so wrong

Actor
_hydrus

SPEED
LIMIT
25
Every storm begins with rain
_hydrus

She was the one
My everything
Loved her so much
Until the sting

Passion ruled
All of our time
We felt so whole
And all was mine

I was only hers
It felt so pure
Muted the demons
She was the cure

The doubts came later
The mind was shocked
I still don't hate her
I am just bad luck

Fumbled
_hydrus

Take the leap
And just give in
Reach out to her
Just to begin

It's been so long
Let's get away
I'll make the plans
For you to stay

We can meet
Redraw the lines
Sketch our paths
Erase the time

Back in your town
I plan to be
Call me back
Let's try to meet

Excuse
_hydrus

ONE WAY
DO NOT ENTER
WRONG WAY

Why must one obey the heart when all it knows is hurt and deceit
_hydrus

Damn this day
It's taking long
Useless thoughts
Of what is wrong

Silence rules
Nothing comes in
I was forgotten
Did anger win

No Reply
_hydrus

Lost in my thoughts is where I become the enemy
_hydrus

Hello
How have you been
I fucking miss you
It all sinks in

So much to say
Words now evade
Heavens voice
Beyond the shade

She answers back
Cosmic the tone
If I could reach
Through this phone

To hold her close
Never let go
Apologize
For what I know

Start all new
Reclaim her heart
Show the life
We did depart

Are you around
Can you be free
She says okay
To an anxious plea

Chance
_hydrus

Every emotion seems so raw when all is awakened with just one call
hydrus

Way back when
There was a life
She was all I knew
Could be my wife

World was ours
We would be wed
Until that night
When she was fed

Discovered clues
Witnessed deceit
Such treachery
How could this be

Disloyal hands
Had made their way
Why understand
Nothing to say

Challenges came
The distance grew
I made my choice
And we were through

Uncovered
_hydrus

Packed my bags
The weekends here
Taking these days
To disappear

I have a plan
Just for this stay
Back in her arms
Repave my way

Playback
_hydrus

I have no map to what awaits...
I only wish to get lost in your escape
_hydrus

This cathedral
Arched in time
Recorded hauntings
Of many crimes

A mansions halls
Traversed and crossed
They bear the names
Of souls we lost

So many tales
Stories of past
Built to scale
Secrets that last

Every room
A gambled feast
Where lives are won
Others deceased

Am I a victor
Or another slave
To strange addictions
Beyond my cave

I set the trap
Will she take the bait
I need to drink
Out of this state

Lobby
_hydrus

_hydrus
Home is not where I live it's where I hide

Darkened wood
Laced in cigar
Timeless flair
For open scars

Every seat
Left drunk alone
A poisoned wall
I call my home

Bar
_hydrus

Waiting just makes me hungrier   _hydrus

Here again
I raise my brow
Her piercing eyes
I know somehow

I recognize
Those subtle lips
A flawless pour
I take a sip

Tended
_hydrus

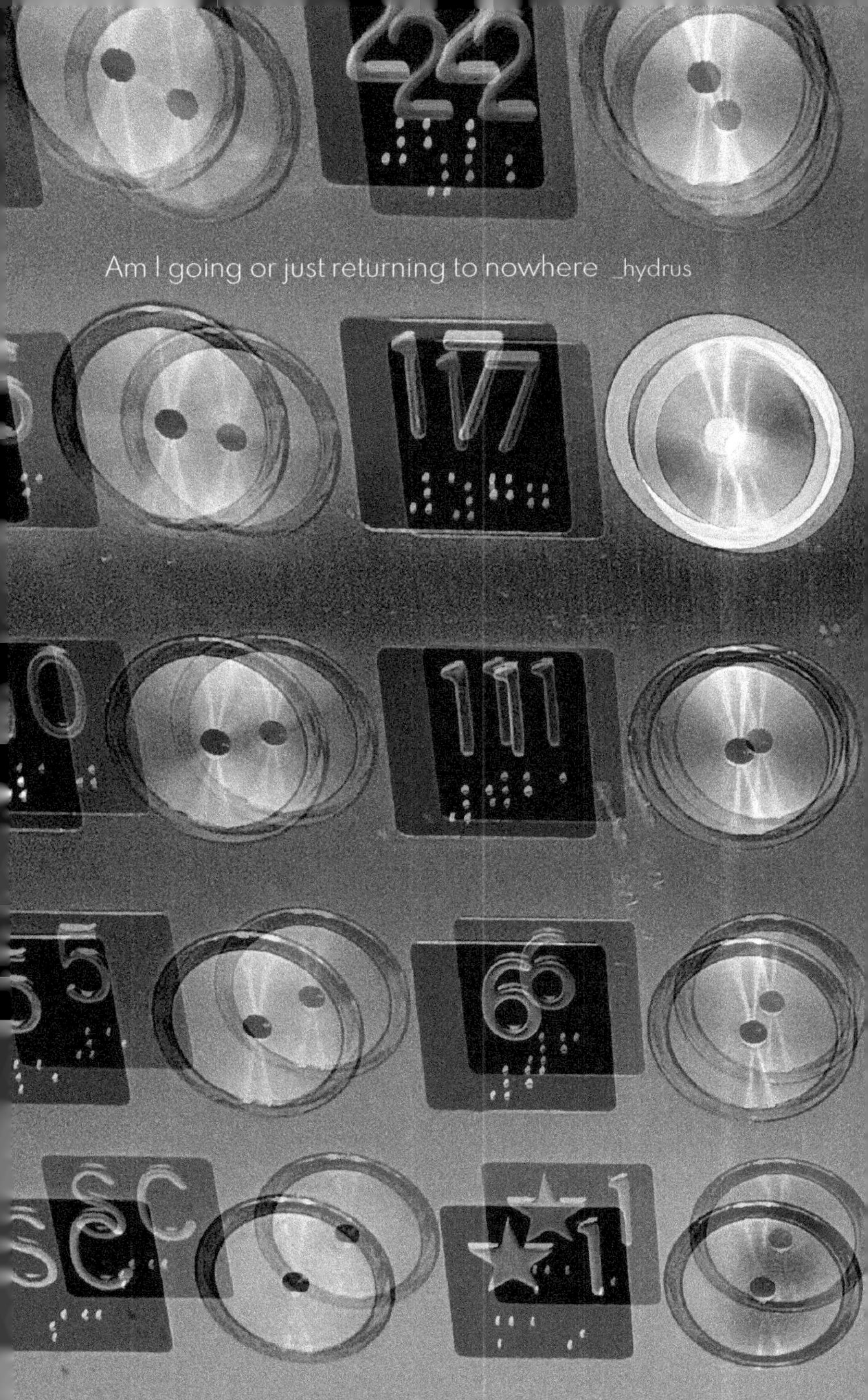
Am I going or just returning to nowhere   _hydrus

Numbers sting
They hurt my eyes
How many drinks
How many lines

This wooden coffin
Planked as I jet
Takes me to heaven
Where I forget

Which way is left
Or is it right
Endless halls
Already night

Step by step
A new routine
I can't forget
It's not a dream

Scrambling keys
I found my grave
The corpse now lays
Inside his cave

Room 2202
_hydrus

I am an expanding crack in a glass filled home _hydrus

Looming eyes
Wall to wall
A cornered prison
For a distant fall

Oak headboards
And tapestry
A refined banquet
Of luxury

Marble accents
Golden decor
Ornate items
Ceiling to floor

Many dungeons
To tie my prey
A fancy cell
Where we all obey

Penthouse
_hydrus

I had to take a chance on forever
When pain was my here and now
_hydrus

Idly waiting
Legs are crossed
An impatient manner
My thoughts are lost

The demons start
To tease the brain
Replay my past
So I relive all pain

Questions rise
To why I'm here
Am I a fool
Trying to reappear

Pretend that magic
Can correct the acts
An illusions play
Without the facts

I knew the ending
And every scene
Including the cast
That ended my dream

Will I be the villain
Or she even show
This is the performance
Together we'll know

Production
_hydrus

Darkness
Awaits
My fate

_hydrus

Doors open
Summer breeze
I feel the warmth
A familiar ease

There she stands
Radiant in place
Pretentious flower
Owning all space

Her hair is flawless
She glides to me
My mouth is vacant
I cannot breathe

Her spell was strong
It had much might
Time had not changed
I could not fight

It grabbed a hold
Of what it claims
Her lips met mine
I felt the chains

Surprise
_hydrus

Ripples sent
Through my bones
Her subtle peck
Ignites my groans

I had forgotten
Such tenderness
A planted kiss
Made me feel blessed

My planned encounter
Had lit the spark
The one that ended
Made life so dark

Can this act
Correct the wrongs
Unite two souls
Rewrite their song

Time will tell
Our lyrics gone
Need new thoughts
Starting with one

Redeemed
_hydrus

BUS ONLY
TRIUM

Retracing my steps only to fall again   _hydrus

Empire state
Where I was born
Steam fountains
And honking horns

Vulgar rants
Served with a slice
Water dogs
Rockefellers ice

Yellow cabs
Walks through the park
Tuxedo nights
Drinks after dark

A thousand stories
Eight million ways
Holding hands
On the subway

Connecting
_hydrus

Every moment
That I am alive
Inside my soul
I have slowly died

Replayed the moments
So full of joy
Until her actions
Woke up the boy

Rewind Play
hydrus

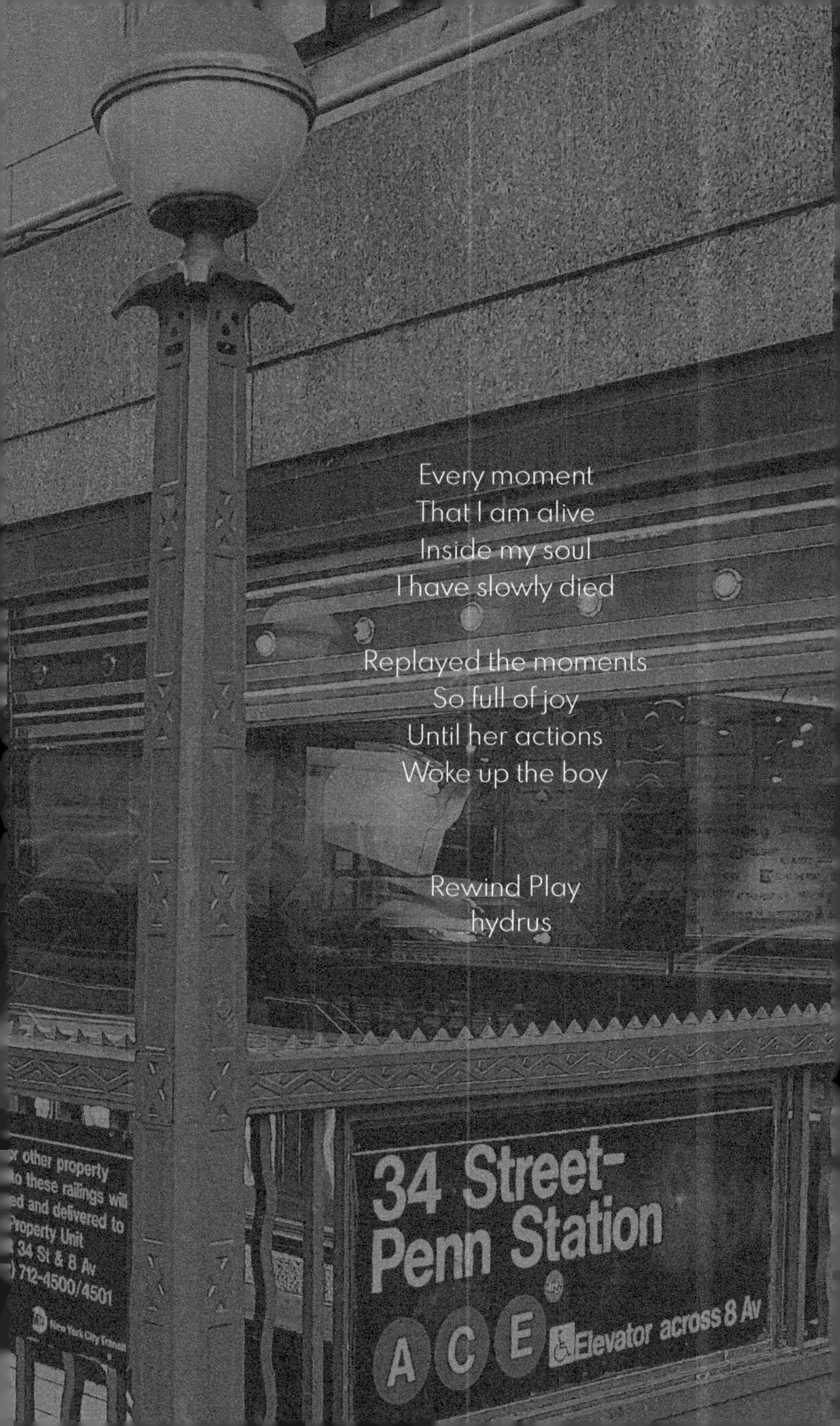

Savage love can overtake the fear one blames for their mistakes _hydrus

Hunger sets
We grab a bite
Catch up on life
Try to unite

We find a booth
Sit side by side
I was all nerves
My mind was fried

She softly spoke
I listened well
Talked of the past
Our heartfelt spell

Confessions came
The truths were told
I took her hand
I felt so bold

We laughed and joked
Eyes gave a glance
I almost choked
Hands tugged my pants

She grinned and smiled
Made me get up
I quickly jumped
It was time to fuck

Diner
_hydrus

Tiled walls
Room for one
We cannot deny
The cravings strong

Pulled me out
Slid me in
Wet her lips
Spread her grin

Slowly stroking
Our bodies met
Reflections pounding
The mirrors sweat

Fingerprints
Make up runs
Digested throat
Her meal is done

Cocktail
_hydrus

Separate ways
She paid the bill
Never got to eat
She took her fill

Dazed footsteps
I find my way
What just happened
I will still pay

Penance
_hydrus

She was my demon
With arctic fire
Cold inside
An a blazed desire

The actions cruel
With one intent
There were no rules
Your love was spent

An addicted muse
Feeding off your pain
A tightening noose
Just all a game

The grip was tight
And claimed your land
Your soul was hers
Under her command

Jacked
_hydrus

Our night always came before morning   _hydrus

Still needing a meal
Now thirsty to drink
The poison must heal
As reality sinks

I sit at the bar
My familiar retreat
Contemplating what happened
Again at my seat

Blur
_hydrus

PILSNER
BLUE
STELLA ARTOIS
BELGIAN WHITE
Heineken
STELLA ARTOIS
GUINNESS
Every drink leads me closer and farther from you _hydrus
Hei

Head in my hands
I feel a tap
Looking up
My drink is capped

I feel her presence
As she appears
It's not the demon
The one I feared

Again this angel
With the flawless pour
I do remember
From the night before

A listened kindness
Mixed and served
Every word
Hit every nerve

Another confession
Reenacting the night
Humored questions
Answered with light

She was my witness
To my heart's appeal
Was this just madness
Was this all real

Pouring
_hydrus

Let me lick every drop
Make your moans never stop

_hydrus

I came here
With a thought in mind
Retrace my steps
To a better time

Looking for happiness
From a place I lost
Feeling the burden
To the lines I crossed

Moving fast
When I've yet to walk
Living sadness
When I forgot to talk

Now these emotions
Haunt me here in bed
Tomorrow waits
Where will I be led

Trap
_hydrus

Alarm sounds off
I jump to start
Open the shades
To erase the dark

Stretch in place
Put on my gear
I need to sweat
Make all thoughts clear

In this temple
I free the mind
Breathe in ideas
Forget all time

My quiet oasis
As muscles flex
Rippled training
Bulged and so tense

Headphones blasting
I feel a tap
It's the angel
From the nightcap

Physical
_hydrus

Workout halted
As I step back
Morning surprise
All dressed in black

This midnight kitten
Has come to train
All of my focus
She now has drained

She takes a look
Begins her routine
Bends all angles
A drunken dream

She hints she's done
Grabs a towel or two
Winks my way
What the world to do

Tempted
_hydrus

Steam rises
As the ripples wave
Conceal her shape
As she swims away

Cloaked in water
Until she reappears
Embraced by beauty
Her tides feel so near

Such a temptress
Did not prepare
For cupids wrath
Leaving me unclear

Thoughts are clouded
Plan lost its view
Alluring serpent
What is one to do

I must walk away
Hiding my tongue
Tonight's the night
There's only one

Proposal
_hydrus

Am I a fool
For letting go
Walking away
From her tempting glow

I saw the look
It pierced through me
She read my mind
I had to flee

Allured
_hydrus

Banded symbol
Etched in haste
Built to cage
Trapped the chase

Chained suspicions
Quiets the crowds
To all who witness
Shouting your vows

A ringed engagement
Etched by birth
Although temptations
Plague my thirst

I must keep focused
As the heavens plea
Taming the fire
On a bended knee

Forged
_hydrus

Car pulls up
With east side class
Onyx black
And tinted glass

The door opens
To a chauffeured dress
Legs are stretched
Style does impress

Cocktails wait
The chariots here
Splashing bubbles
As we drink and cheer

Soon we kiss
We are on our way
The second night
To an endless stay

Course
_hydrus

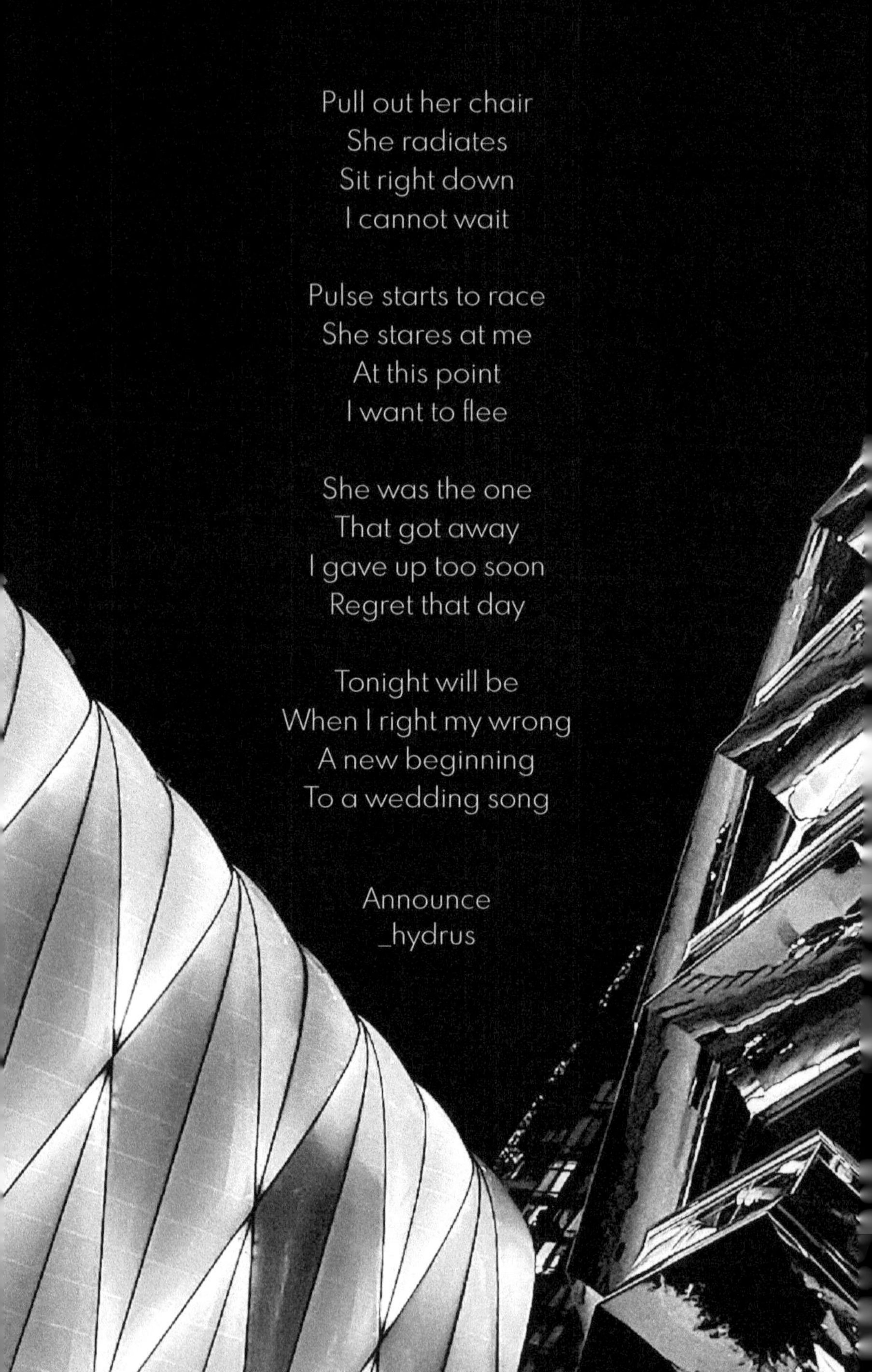

Pull out her chair
She radiates
Sit right down
I cannot wait

Pulse starts to race
She stares at me
At this point
I want to flee

She was the one
That got away
I gave up too soon
Regret that day

Tonight will be
When I right my wrong
A new beginning
To a wedding song

Announce
_hydrus

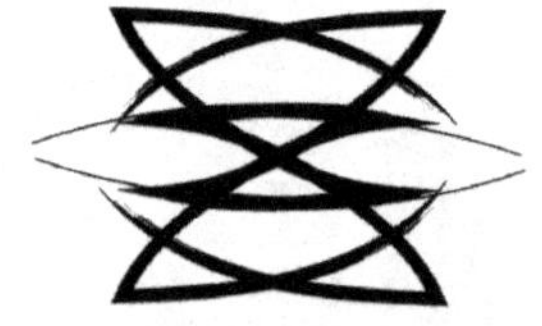

Heart beats
It skips and stirs
An unintelligible mess
I can't find the words

Marry me
Make me your man
Let's resume our story
And our life as planned

Yes
_hydrus

A caressing kiss
On one knee
Her heart is mine
I'm full of glee

We celebrate
Having our wine
Finish the meal
Rejoiced and dined

In her arms
A perfect night
The devils gone
As we unite

I'm such a fool
To live my life
Without this girl
To be my wife

Success
_hydrus

We make our way
Back to my nest
Hungers raw
We will not rest

Mirrored ceilings
Adorn the sky
Watching us
And her blissful eyes

I never want
To leave her side
Our secrets dark
Nowhere left to hide

Feral
_hydrus

How high do you have to be to watch yourself falling
_hydrus

She wrapped her thighs
Around his waist
Showing him
What he could taste

Devilish grins
And subtle looks
Turned to groans
As fingers took

Slowly feeling
What he craved
She gave him bliss
And all her waves

He drank her all
She quietly came
Whispering a
Forgotten name

Shock
_hydrus

Betrayal

_hydrus

The name she moaned
It was also known
Her fingers trembled
A voice now groaned

How could this be
Such troubled shame
Blind fantasy
My trust to blame

Stranger
_hydrus

Tell me the truth
After what we did
All your lies
And all you hid

It doesn't matter
It's all the same
Leave me now
Take all I came

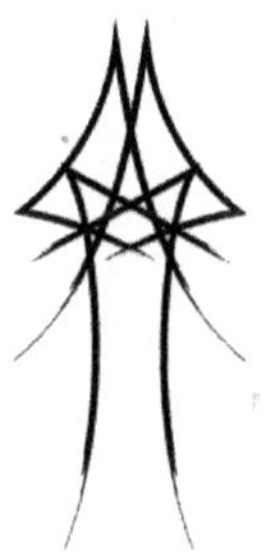

Confrontation
_hydrus

Every time
That we speak
I fall in love
Become so weak

My heart grows full
And then it dies
You are with him
You cannot lie

Shame
_hydrus

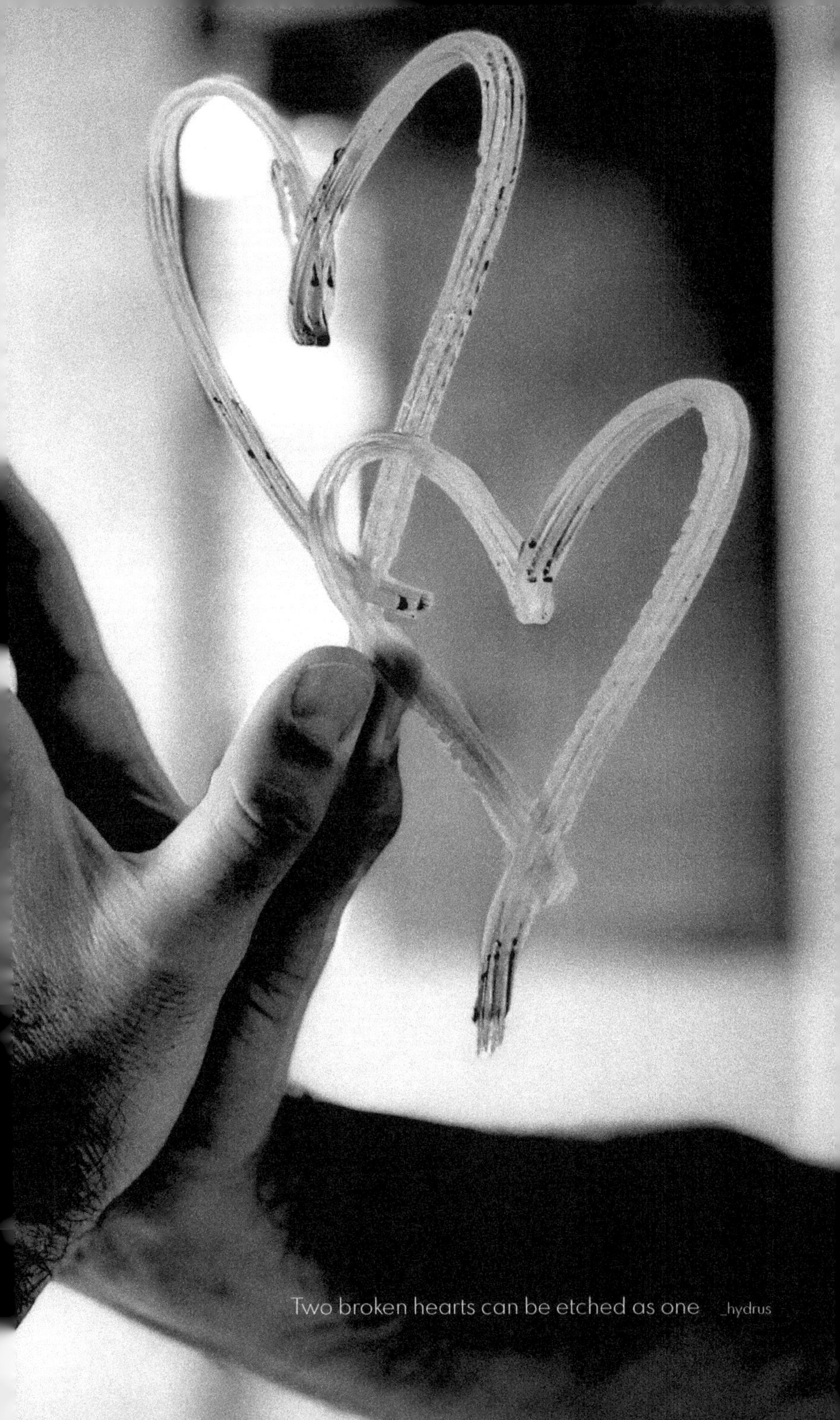
Two broken hearts can be etched as one   _hydrus

All this time
It was a game
I only knew
Once you came

Our sweaty mess
Our bodies one
I was not enough
Now we are done

Quell
_hydrus

_As I sit
In agony
I think of her
And what could be

Memories made
Each moment etched
It was so new
Not so far fetched

We grew as one
Our bond was tight
Every word meant
It felt so right

Now in the calm
Playing the past
I missed the signs
We could not last

Hints
_hydrus

Remember the time
You surprised me at work
Caught me off guard
I was such a jerk

Instead of passion
I became enraged
These were my actions
So disengaged

Cruel and boisterous
A crimson fool
An erratic asshole
No time to cool

Such violent wrath
Anger sublime
A rotting apple
This marked the time

Hollowed
_hydrus

Only in my thoughts can you seem uncruel _hydrus

Days have ended
The suns now alive
Time has flown
The past has died

No longer wielding
A fiery ax
Faith has changed me
I removed my mask

Rendered
_hydrus

Beyond this horizon
Beats my beginning
_hydrus

Paint me in your scent and frame me where I hang   _hydrus

All these thoughts
That drown in me
A fevered nightmare
I grieve constantly

Replaying the moments
The good and bad
So many questions
That I never had

Which was the moment
Where you felt betrayed
Before was silence
Now storms the rage

The earth now trembles
Vanished remorse
I must reassemble
To correct my course

Woke
_hydrus

Broken walls
Shredded shelves
Torn out pages
Where the devils delve

This burning madness
We called a home
I will set on fire
Bury your bones

Start again
Find my way
Erase the voices
That always play

Regain my path
Find my course
Retake the losses
All by force

Scorch
_hydrus

My mind wanders
It aimlessly leads
I try to think of goodness
But madness selfishly bleeds

The sun shined
As my eyes burned
A sleepless night
Nothing was learned

I woke right up
Another man
Transformed by fate
Needing a plan

Trying to live
Finding my soul
One that will give
Not to control

So much was done
But here I stand
Another day
Not in command

Risen
_hydrus

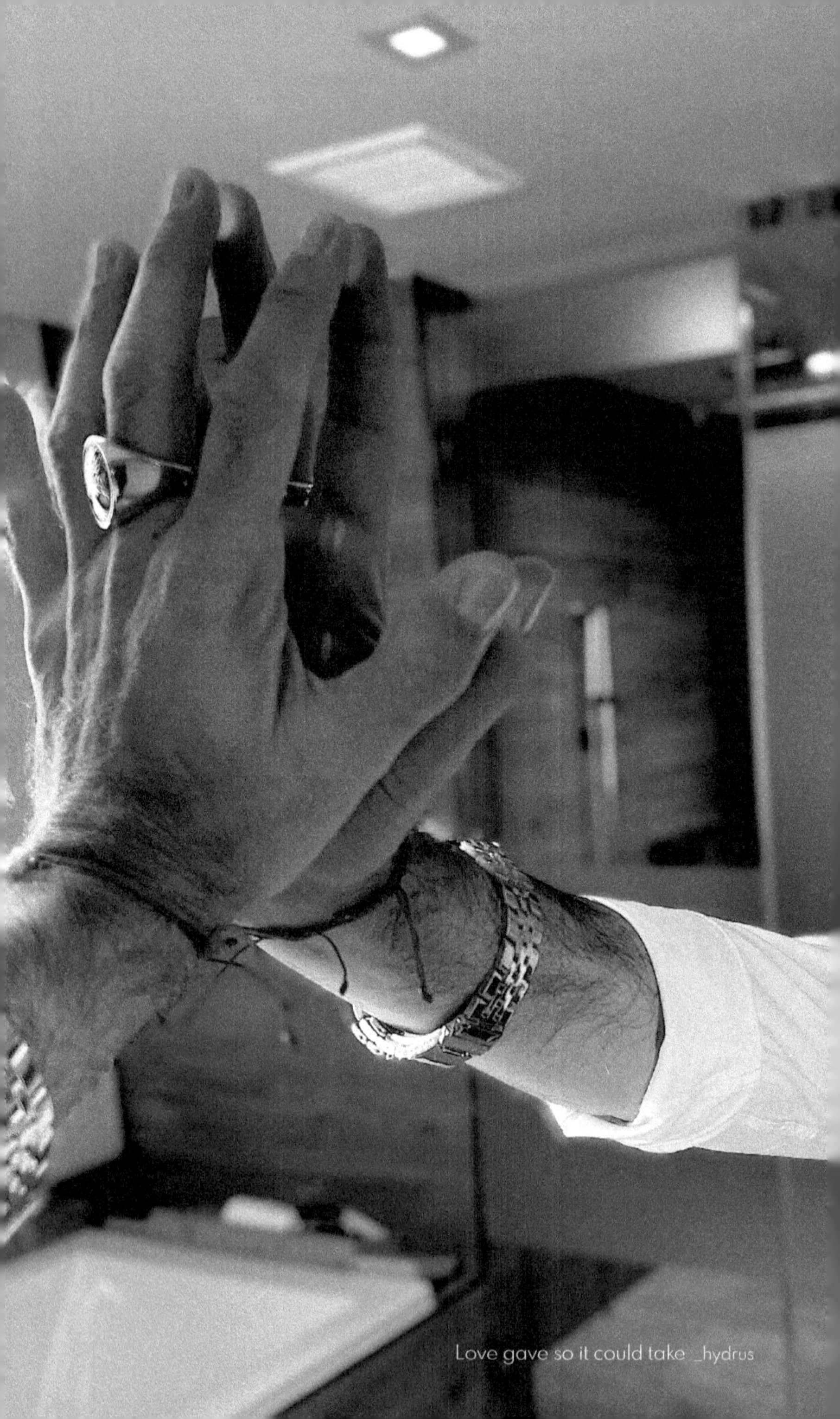
Love gave so it could take _hydrus

Loneliness taunts
As my shadow hides
Nothing to flaunt
Emotions still high

Eerie sounds
That silence makes
Breaks my heart
Keeps me awake

Walls closing in
As demons crawl
Covered eyes
The tears just fall

No one around
I can't retreat
The thoughts appear
I feel defeat

Parted
_hydrus

Phone rings
Is it a sign
Quiet the noises
That made me blind

Could this be
An angels call
Another chance
To find it all

What can I answer
Who will recite
Give me answers
To sleep at night

I find the courage
To hear a voice
A sounding trumpet
Her thirsty voice

Lurking
_hydrus

I took the bait
My hungers real
The tide was red
From the blood we spilled

This scarlet ocean
Where I once had drowned
Has reclaimed my life
Never to be found

Surfaced
_hydrus

Imagination ran
Thought I heard wings
But it was not
Only the devil sings

Trumpets
_hydrus

Black leather
A strapless flaunt
Wicked the trance
Inside this haunt

The devils here
Reaping for fun
An ageless laughter
Her minds her gun

Sharpened talons
Conceal the flood
The cravings thirsty
For all my blood

There's nothing gentle
The spells are cast
Will I be broken
I'm hers at last

Studded
_hydrus

Keys in hand
We go upstairs
So unafraid
So unaware

I grab her hands
Our bodies pressed
She feels me throb
Undo her dress

She bites my neck
To drink my veins
Our tongues now meet
Numb to the pain

Inside I grow
Filling her nest
The moans are low
This was a test

My muscles wet
The legs apart
Our rivers met
To retake the heart

Ambushed
_hydrus

Every thrust
Every pain
Was choked away
As I was drained

_hydrus

I surrendered
To her every touch
Became obedient
Love was too much

Greed ruled passion
She had the skills
The thirst was violent
Choking to thrill

Aroused submission
And a taste for pain
Our bodies one
As I drank her rain

There were no limits
Rules would not apply
I was all she wanted
That would be a lie

Talent
_hydrus

Wild untamed
She rode her beast
Screams exclaimed
He filled her seat

Passions brewed
There was no fight
Seduction grew
All through the night

Swallowed tongues
Sweat on backs
Tangled hair
Flesh attacks

Wrestled sheets
With mangled skin
Clenching tight
As I am pinned

Pounding headboards
Nails dig in
A marked assassin
She claimed my sin

Handled
_hydrus

Even my reflection judges me _hydrus

Another horizon
Through glared filled glass
Has left me speechless
As the morning past

Drunken eyes
My hands search in vain
A printed note
With a scribbled name

Bye
_hydrus

EXIT
Gone only to remain   _hydrus

Dear heartache
I have returned
You signed your life
Once again to burn

I brought the matches
And you lit a fire
This one encounter
To reignite desire

You were so whole
Filling me so well
Dripping bliss
But no one can tell

Keep our secret
Our romance will thrive
Destiny found us
You cannot hide

Sincerely
_hydrus

Life so cruel
In its joking way
It took my life
And all my days

I had to battle
Fight my own will
Nagging voices
That made me kill

Relentless torture
Of a haunted past
Chased the child
That would never last

How many bodies
Endless their stares
I was the weapon
Now no one cares

Enlisted
_hydrus

The drive feels endless
On a roadless map
So much confusion
To again be trapped

Stop lights blinking
As I miss my turn
Surrounding cliffs
Sliding off to burn

Downfall
_hydrus

So far away from who I thought I could be   _hydrus

Pounding raindrops
Thunder screams
Awake once more
From this constant dream

No more illusions
The laughters gone
Turning dials
As I find our song

Constant torment
Why you left my side
Abandoned highways
For this troubled ride

Neon blinking
For a vacant heart
The motels empty
Ending my start

Parked
_hydrus

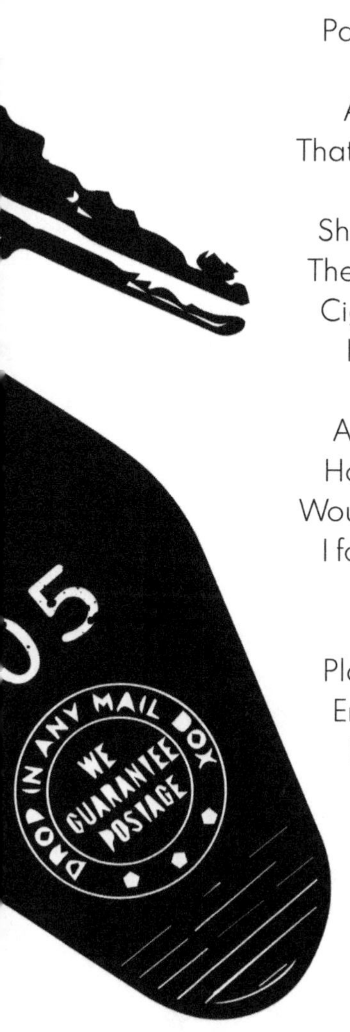

Painted wallpaper
Dim the lights
A banging wall
That reminds our night

Sheets are tattered
They engulf the trash
Cigarettes burning
I ingest the ash

A clouded shield
Hovers to conceal
Wounds are bleeding
I forgot what's real

All alone
Plagued the score
Empty beer cans
Dress the floor

Habitual
_hydrus

Dressers blessed
With a crumpled life
Wallet thrown
A pocket knife

Set of keys
Crush a benjamin
Scribbled numbers
A kissed napkin

Reminder
_hydrus

Closing walls
The ceiling falls
Crushed again
It was my call

I will now run
Into the night
Ride my bike
Fade out of site

Hit the highway
At full speed
As the winds
Erase my deeds

With any luck
Something I lack
Never saw the truck
I'm on my back

Lights
_hydrus

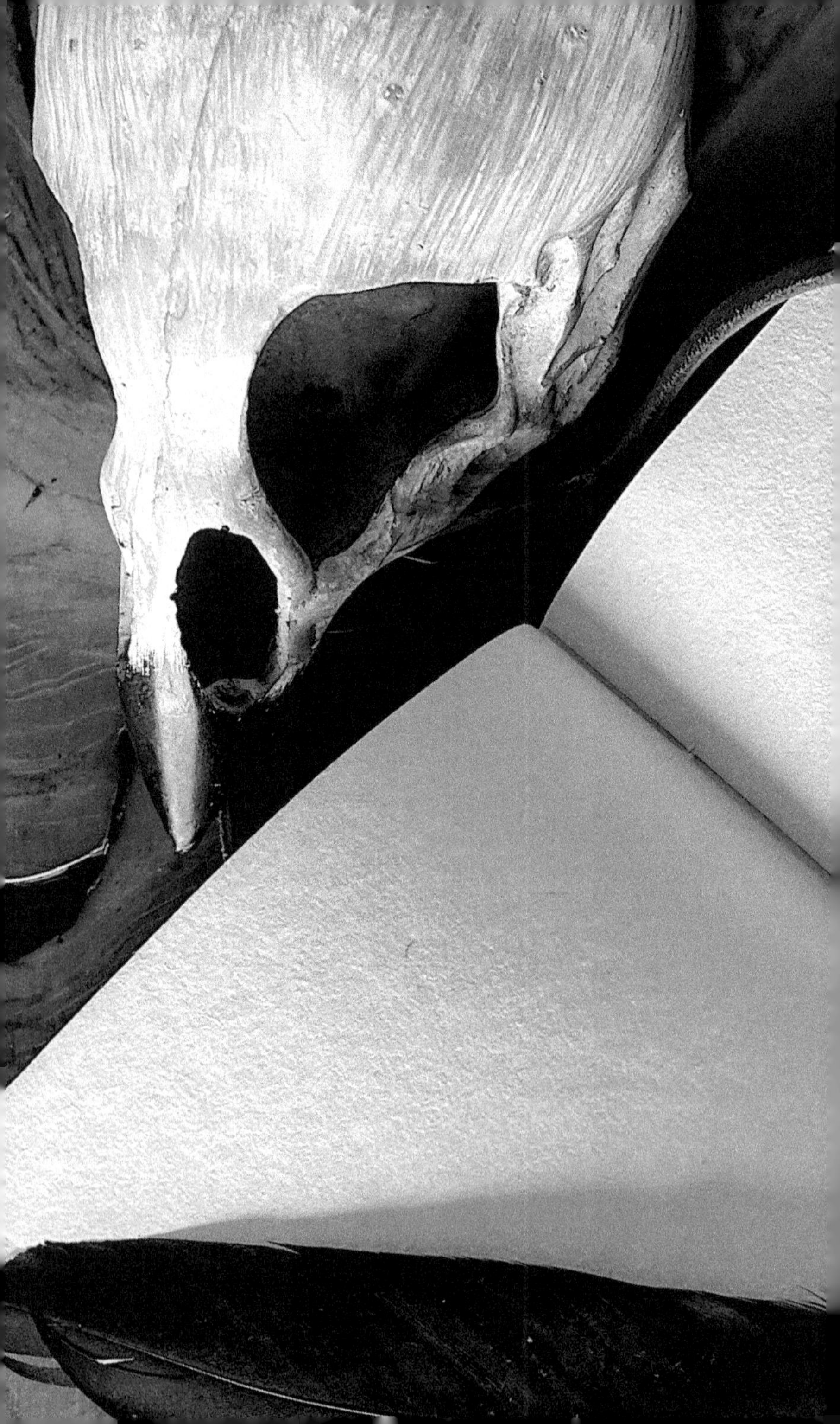

EYES ARE CLOSED
UNDER THIS MASK
COMMANDS ARE MOANED
SHE KNOWS HER TASK

CANNOT MOVE
MY HANDS ARE BOUND
I FEEL HER LIPS
I'M UPSIDE DOWN

_hydrus

... To Be Continued

A FALLEND SERIES **BOOK TWO**

BROKEND

_HYDRUS

December 2022

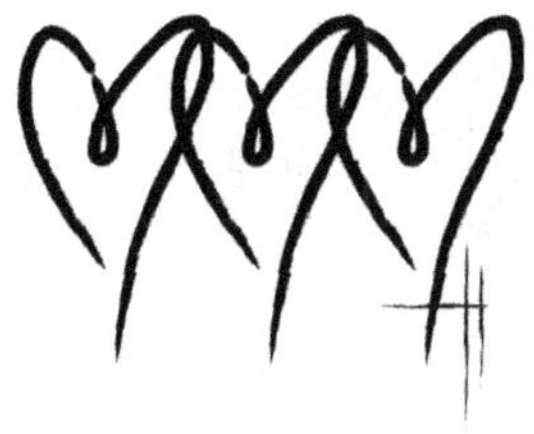

I smiled for what I had to fear
Edgar Allan Poe

Thank You

Thank you to all my readers!
I am so thankful to all of you that take time to read
my words and share in my story. Thank you all
again for all your love and support. I only wish to
touch each of your hearts as your continuing support
has touched mine.

Thank you to my incredible team!
(Cleo & Jojo)
For all of your hard work and tireless support. You
are the engines behind Hydrus and I am very
grateful and lucky to be able to work with both of
you.

Thank you to all the ravens for your continuing
love and support. For being such a big part of this
journey and for always making time to make me a
small part of your lives.

WEAK**END**

Playlist

Call Out My Name	The Weeknd
Someone You Loved	Lewis Capaldi
Lost in the Fire	Gesaffelstein, The Weeknd
Summertime Sadness	Lana Del Rey
Circles	Post Malone
Middle Of The Night	Elley Duhè
Control	Zoe Wees
I Feel Like I'm Drowning	Two Feet
Remember	PLAZA
Fahrenheit	Azee
love is evil	Dxvn, Daniel Di Angelo
Bad Drugs	King Kavalier, ChrisLee
Lie To Me	Black Atlass
Where's My Love	SYML
Never Enough	Black Atlass
Sacrifice	Black Atlass, Jessie Reyez
Silence	Marshmello, Khalid
Stay	Rihanna, Mikky Ekko
Naked	James Arthur
Let It Go	James Bay
Heartless	Kanye West

Listen here:
https://spoti.fi/3TlxOXO

Also by: _hydrus

ENDVISIBLE

A collection of poems about the endless feeling of being invisible while going through the emotions and sometimes cruelties of life. Illustrated by the author's own photography, this book guides us through grief, loss and love in a dark and inspiring way typical to how Hydrus's writing helps us cope with reality.

AWAK**END**

Tarots cards, much like poems, have the ability to paint a vivid picture of what once was or what could be. They delve into the subtleties that we all carry within ourselves and the secrets that make us who we are.

AwakEND is an immersion into the world of tarot and its mysteries. Read it one way, then another, and let the words guide you into the meaning of each card.
Allow chance and curiosity to accompany you on this incredible journey and let your heart awaken to hope even after having thought everything was lost...

And who knows what secrets you might find out about yourself...

DARK**END**

Is a small look into the world I call my reality.

Through poems, photography and art, I try to capture the ups and downs of this voyage we call life, and sometimes I refer to it as just existing.

Embedded in my words are stories of emotions and feelings that range from the darkest of moments to times of having some type of hope for resolve.

Life is raw and ever-evolving, and we always seem to put ourselves last overall. Time proves to be quite relentless. I hope that we all find common ground through our everyday struggles and in the end, understand that love, although painful at times, can provide so many answers.

So the question then becomes "how can we better love ourselves?"

HEART**END**

Is about how we experience love and some of the journeys we embark on when love strikes our heart. It's about the numerous complex phases and ever changing stages of the purest human emotions.

It might be a first kiss, a new romance, a guilty pleasure or a sense of loss but love always helps us reach the heavens or crash down upon its shores.

Love gives even when it takes, it heals and embeds its mark and sculpts us into who we are.

"We all open our hearts and in the end this is the love we bleed."
_hydrus

ENDTHOLOGY

Is a collection of poems drawn up from experiences, thoughts, and emotions. Not everything in the world is dark, but many times we live without any light. We lose ourselves in what we consider our reality. Our souls forget what is important. At the same time, we rejoice when we regain our passion and our inner light.

We might live many lives, but which one will you always remember?

What memories will we ink?

What will have true meaning?

How will we live our END?

_hydrus

A collection of poems that deal with the human struggle of being in love. The emotional roller coaster and the ups and downs that our souls take on this journey. This path is one of endless bliss but some-times agony.

Love is always a conflict of raw emotion and trust. It is a journey we seek to take and at times we regret we do. It is a struggle between good vs. evil but mostly in ourselves.

ENDROAD

An original collection of poetry, comprised of new works, writings, and photography. It documents the many facets of ones inner journey. It deals with our ever-changing emotions, and how the mind and heart react differently when confronted by lifes cruel ironies.

We all live inside and outside ourselves. The quiet whispers we hear and the ones we ignore. The inner voice that makes us passionate, gives us hope, or creates the monster that sharpens their teeth.

ENDroad details the winding aspects of that search for answers. It shows that we all sometimes feel the same. That we are not alone. The paths we take or the ones that take us to mold our humanity into who we are. Each one presents us with the ability for us to rediscover ourselves again.

At times we might feel lost but the truth to finding our way will always rest in our hearts.

My end does not mean I am finished
It only reveals that I am starting again.
_hydrus

About The Author

Anonymous poet, photographer and artist,
Hydrus documents through his poems the darkness and the
glimmers of life taunting us when we are in the shadows,
as well as many of the little things which make a colossal impact
on who we are.

Connect with _hydrus:

Website: www.hydruspoetry.com
Instagram: @hydruspoetry
Facebook: www.facebook.com/hydruspoetry
TikTok: @hydrus_ravens
Redbubble Merchandise:
www.redbubble.com/people/hydruspoetry/explore

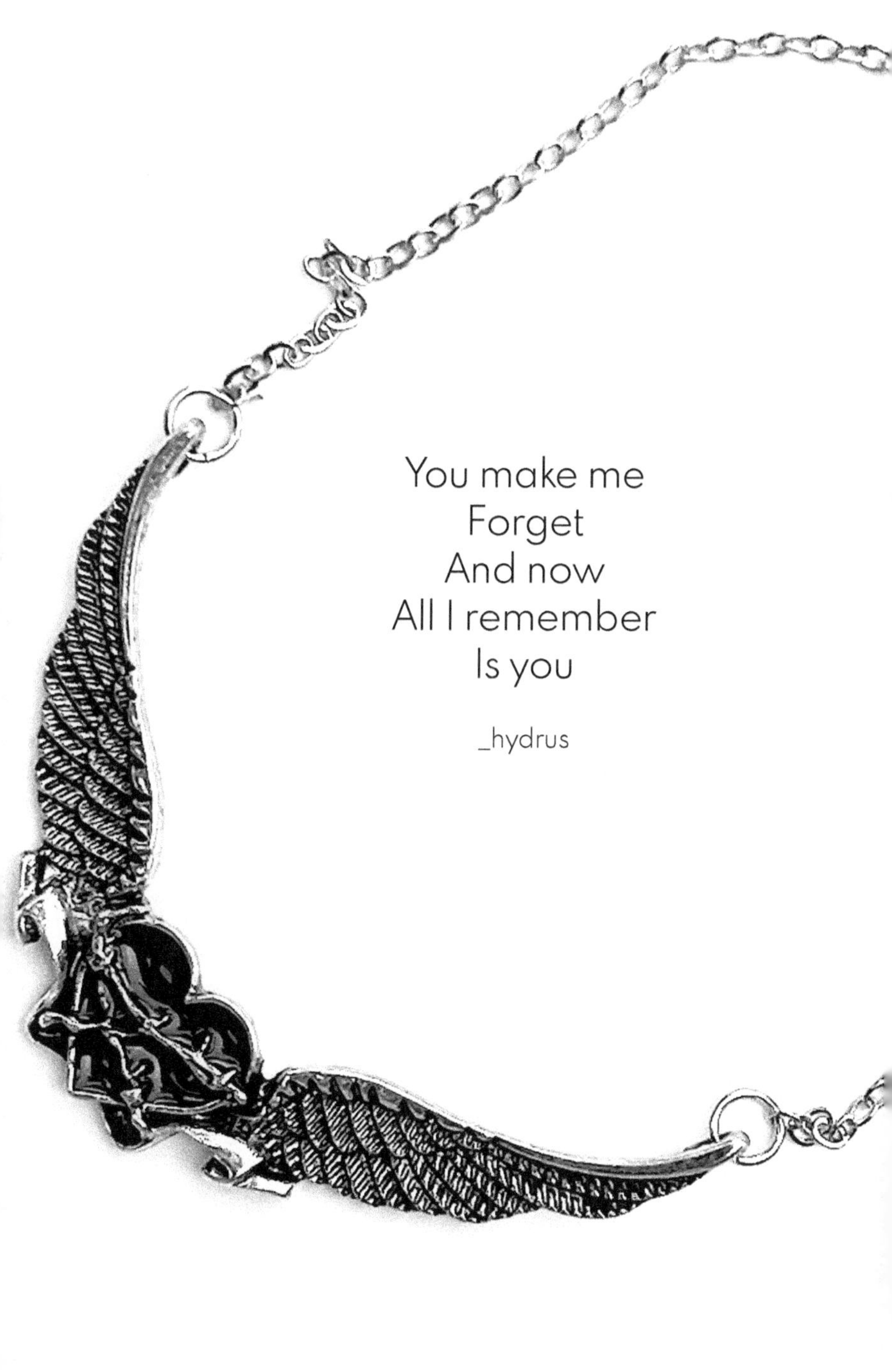
You make me
Forget
And now
All I remember
Is you

_hydrus